A Heavenly World

Tracey Dean Widelitz

Illustrated by Jennifer Sara Widelitz

NEWMAN SPRINGS PUBLISHING
320 Broad Street
Red Bank, NJ 07701

First originally published by Newman Springs Publishing 2022

ISBN 978-1-63881-445-0 (Paperback)
ISBN 978-1-63881-446-7 (Digital)

Printed in the United States of America

To

Precious,

Sweetie,

Savannah,

and

Juliet

To whom is your book dedicated?

_____

There is another beautiful world
where puppies roam free,

lazily playing, romping, or rolling under a leafy shade tree.

Flying, soaring, running
free and wild

3

until they are needed for another
human, especially a child.

They enter our lives to fulfill their purpose or need,

5

giving us unconditional
love, undeniable protection,
and all without greed.

Loving tummy
rubs,

7

warm snuggles,

and endless kisses—

Tracey's ICE CREAM

ICE CREAM:
CHOCOLATE
VANILLA
STRAWBERRY

DOG-FRIENDLY
ICE CREAM
AVAILABLE!

my dog completely
fulfills my life

10

through all of
life's hits

11

and misses.

I will be with you, from when you are my puppy

until you are old and gray,

because even though you will eventually leave, I know that you will truly never go away.

Because...

there is another beautiful world where puppies roam free.

18

About the Author

A *Heavenly World* is Tracey Dean Widelitz's first children's book. Tracey is the mother to two beautiful daughters, but her inspiration for this book was from her beloved fur-baby Precious, who crossed over the rainbow bridge too soon. Tracey also loves writing poetry, photography, and sketching, and absolutely loves getting puppy kisses from her newest fur-baby Honey Bun

CPSIA information can be obtained
at www.ICGtesting.com
Printed in the USA
LVRC082153140522
718475LV00003B/130

9 781638 814450